THE BIG SNEEZE

Story by
H. E. TODD

Pictures by
VAL BIRO

KNIGHT BOOKS
Hodder and Stoughton

In the middle of the night on Christmas Eve Bobby
Brewster was wakened by a loud sneeze – "ATISHOO!"
  At first he thought it was part of a dream, but then
he heard it again – "ATISHOO!"

He switched on his bedside light, and sitting on the chair was an old gentleman with a white beard, dressed in a red coat with a red hood on his head.

"Who are you?" asked Bobby. That was a silly question, wasn't it?

"I'm Father Christmas," answered the man – "ATISHOO!"

"The *real* Father Christmas?" asked Bobby.

"Yes" said the man – "ATISHOO!"

"You have a horrid cold," said Bobby.

"I don't feel at all well," said Father Christmas – "ATISHOO!"

The sneeze was so loud that it brought Bobby's mother and father into the room, too!

As soon as Mrs Brewster saw who was there with Bobby she said:

"Why Father Christmas, you poor old gentleman, you don't look at all well."

"ATISHOO!" sneezed Father Christmas.

Then Mr Brewster looked outside. It was snowing hard.

"You can't go out on a night like this with a cold like that," he said.

"What about my p-p-p-presents?" asked Father Christmas – "ATISHOO!"

"*We* will deliver your presents for you," said Mr Brewster. "You must go to bed."

So Mrs Brewster filled a nice hot water bottle. Mr Brewster turned on the gas fire in the spare bedroom.

Bobby fetched a pair of his father's pyjamas from the chest of drawers. Then they helped Father Christmas to undress. Got him into bed. Put the hot water bottle in with him. Tucked him up. Put his beard over the top of the bedclothes to make him all the warmer. And he went to sleep.

"Mother must stay indoors in case Father Christmas wakes up and wants something," said Mr Brewster. "Bobby, *you* must come and help me deliver the presents."

Bobby felt very important. It was half past one in the morning! He put on his warm clothes, and they went outside.

Standing there were
a reindeer and sledge.

On the back seat of the sledge were a pile of parcels and a pile of labels. They were just going to look at them when the reindeer turned his head round and demanded "Hi, what are you doing?"

"We're going to deliver the presents," explained Mr Brewster. "Father Christmas has gone to bed with a cold."

"I might have guessed it," said the reindeer. "He can be a silly old man at times you know. We told him his cold was getting worse but he insisted on carrying on. Luckily he nearly finished, but he didn't have time to tie on all the labels, so if you will please tie the top labels to the top parcels in order, I will tell you where to deliver them."

Off they went. He was a very clever reindeer and knew exactly where to go. Mr Brewster wondered whether he was supposed to climb on the roofs and down the chimneys, but the reindeer said "No, you're not used to it. You might get stuck. Leave the parcels in the porches."

There was one anxious moment. They thought they had run out of labels – but they found some lying on the floor of the sledge, so they tied them on, delivered the parcels, and then went home.

Then they wondered what to do with the reindeer. He could not get in the front door because his horns were too wide. Luckily the garage was empty because their car was being mended, so they fetched some cushions and the reindeer was able to sleep in there.

"Leave the garage door ajar," he said, "in case Father Christmas wakes up and feels better and wants to go home in the night."

By then it was half past two. They were both tired out so they went up to bed and fell straight off to sleep.

When Bobby woke up in the morning he was excited. Christmas Day! He wondered what had happened to Father Christmas, and when he went into the spare bedroom the bed was empty. But Father Christmas had left a note.

Dear Brewsters,
Thank you for being so kind to me and my reindeer. I feel much better and since waking up have not once sneezed ATISHOO, so I have gone home.
A very Happy Christmas to you all,

Love from
Father Christmas

That is not quite the end of the story. On Christmas morning they went to visit Grandfather Brewster after Church. On the way, they met an elderly lady.

"A Happy Christmas, Mrs Neilson," said Bobby. "Did you get a nice Christmas present?"

"Well, it's all right," she replied. "But I don't think I shall ever use it. It's a box of cigars!"

"That's nothing," said Mr Harrison, looking over his garden fence, "my wife was given a pair of football boots. My daughter was given a razor. My son was given a bottle of scent. And do you know what I got? A frilly nightdress!"

"We must have muddled things up,"
Mr Brewster said to Bobby. There was
no doubt about it –

An old gentleman aged
ninety-seven had a baby's
rattle and a baby of nine
months had an
Encyclopaedia!

They were worried about Grandfather Brewster – but they need not have been. When they rang his bell he came to the front door and cried "A Happy Christmas.

I have been given the best Christmas present I ever had in my life. Come in and look."

They went into the sitting room, and all round the floor was the track of an electric train set.

"I've wanted one of these since I was a boy," said Grandfather Brewster, "and now I've got it."

And he pulled the switch and the engine and carriages went whizzing round the track!

On Boxing night the Brewsters arranged a special party and invited the neighbours. They all came and brought their Christmas presents. Everyone had a lovely time, and before leaving they exchanged their presents so that each person had what he or she wanted.

Luckily a boy badly wanted the flashing torch which had been meant for Grandfather Brewster, so Grandfather was able to keep his electric trains.

And he plays with them every day.

British Library Cataloguing in Publication Data
Todd, H. E.
The big sneeze
I. Title 2. Biro, Val
823'.914[J]   PZ7

ISBN 0-340-39895-7

Text copyright © 1980 H. E. Todd
Illustrations copyright © 1980 Val Biro

First published by Hodder and Stoughton 1980
This edition first published by Knight Books 1986
Second impression 1987

Printed and bound in Hong Kong for
Hodder and Stoughton Paperbacks
a division of Hodder and Stoughton Ltd,
Mill Road, Dunton Green, Sevenoaks, Kent TN13 2YJ
(Editorial Office: 47 Bedford Square, London WC1B 3DP)